This book belongs to

Richard Boiteau
6/1/90

Reina

Hansel
and
Gretel

BARRON'S
New York. Toronto

Once upon a time, there was a poor woodcutter who lived with his wife and two children in a land where hard times had fallen. There was no one to buy the wood he chopped, and food was becoming scarce. One night he told his wife that he was worried that the four of them would not be able to survive because they were so poor and had too many mouths to feed. He didn't know what to do.

Meanwhile, Hansel and Gretel, their two children, were awake in the next room and had overheard their conversation. They felt that they were a burden to their parents, and decided to run away.

They set off into the dark night and were very frightened.
Hansel told Gretel not to worry, that he would take care of her.
As they walked along the path, Hansel broke off bits of bread
they had taken from home, and he dropped them so they would
know the direction they had come from, in case they had to go

back. They soon became very cold and tired, and wondered if they should return. After several hours, they decided they wanted to go back—but it was too late. The birds had eaten the crumbs, and now they were truly lost.

Gretel began to cry.

Suddenly, they came across a strange house made of gingerbread and cakes. It was covered with cookies, and vanilla frosting, and candy! Hansel and Gretel squealed with delight. They ran over to the house and started to break off pieces and eat them.

Then they heard the voice of an old woman, saying, "Who's that nibbling at my house? You must be hungry, little mice. Won't you come in and have something to eat? Then you can rest yourselves."

The old woman's voice sounded so friendly, and they were so tired and hungry, that they went inside.

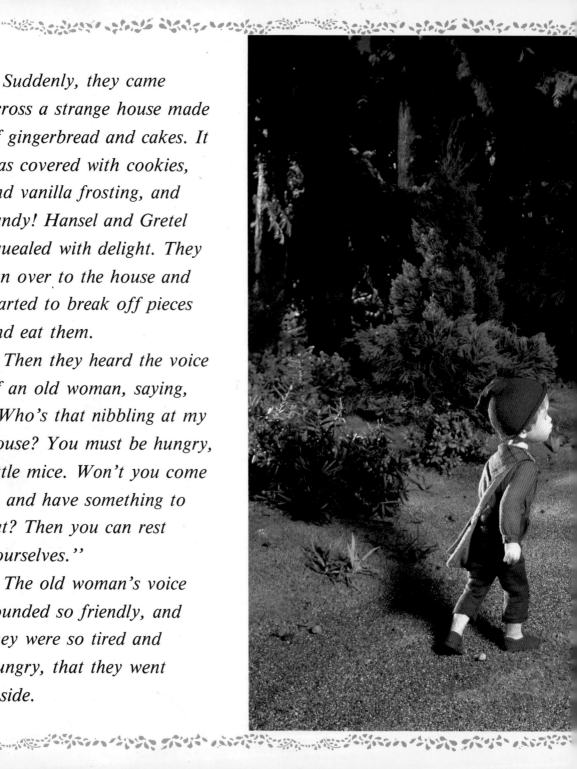

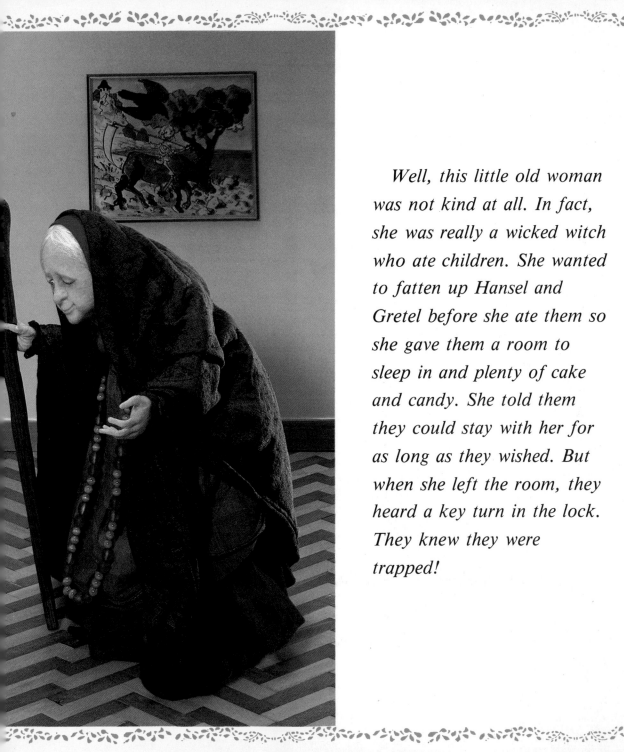

Well, this little old woman was not kind at all. In fact, she was really a wicked witch who ate children. She wanted to fatten up Hansel and Gretel before she ate them so she gave them a room to sleep in and plenty of cake and candy. She told them they could stay with her for as long as they wished. But when she left the room, they heard a key turn in the lock. They knew they were trapped!

The witch decided that Hansel was the fatter of the two. She decided to put him in a cage and feed him as much as possible. If Hansel were in a cage, then Gretel wouldn't try to escape.

Since the witch could not see very well, she asked Hansel to stick out his finger so she could feel how fat he was getting. But Hansel tricked the witch by holding out a chicken bone. This fooled the witch for some time. However, she became impatient when it appeared that he was not getting any plumper. So she decided to eat him anyway.

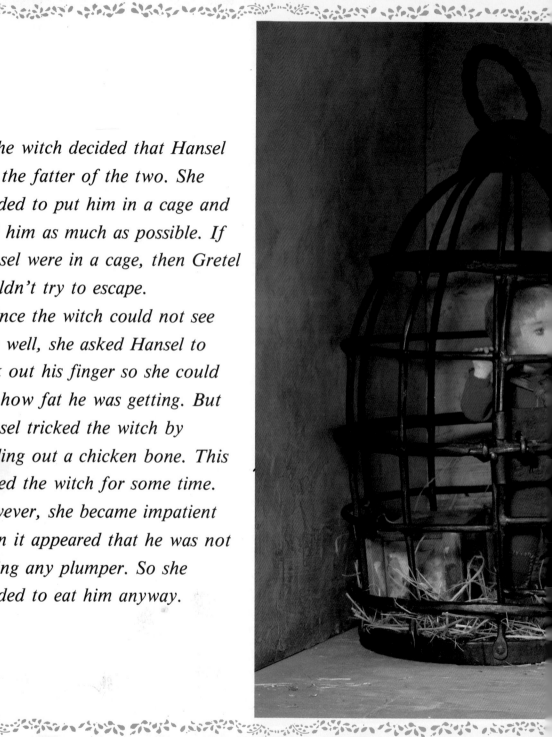

She made poor Gretel gather wood to build the fire in which she was going to cook Hansel. Gretel had no choice but to do as she was told.

As the witch had poor eyesight, she asked Gretel to
check if the fire was ready. Gretel replied that it was not.
Again the witch asked if it was ready. Again Gretel said
that it was not.

The witch was getting anxious to have her dinner so she decided to check for herself. She opened the oven door and poked her head inside. Just at that moment, Gretel pushed the witch, who toppled into the oven head first!

Gretel locked the oven door, and the witch went up in smoke. Then Gretel let Hansel out of the cage, and they went around the house, gathering food and many gold coins they had found.

They wandered around the forest for several hours, looking for their cottage. Finally, they found a familiar area and soon they found their cottage. Their mother and father were overjoyed to see them. They didn't know why they had left, and they were very upset. They hugged their children joyfully. Then Hansel and Gretel took out the gold coins they had taken from the witch's house and all four of them rejoiced that they would never again go hungry.

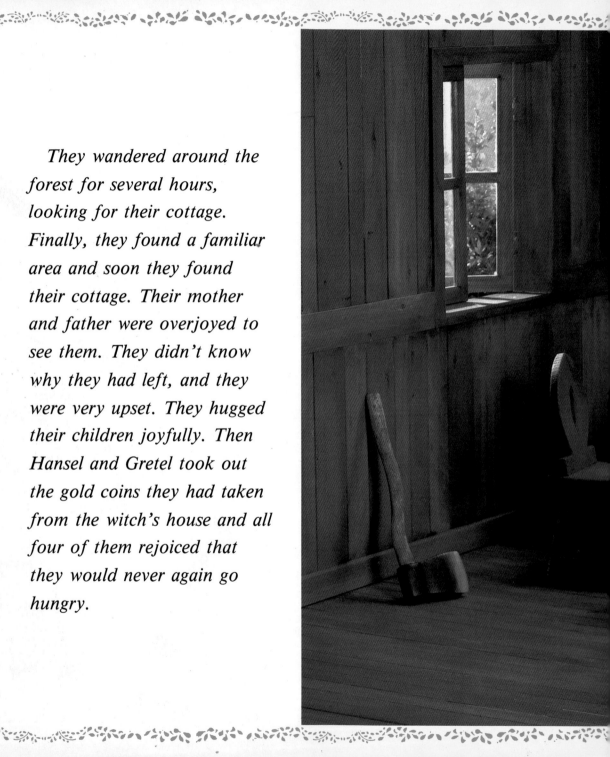